HODDER CHILDREN'S BOOKS

First published in Great Britain in 2021 by Hodder & Stoughton

10 9 8 7 6 5 4 3 2 1

A CIP catalogue record for this book is available from the British Library.

ISBN 978 1 444 95796 9

Printed and bound in China.

The paper and board used in this book are made from wood from responsible sources.

MIX
Paper from
responsible sources
FSC® C104740
FSC
www.fsc.org

Hodder Children's Books
An imprint of
Hachette Children's Group
Part of Hodder & Stoughton
Carmelite House
50 Victoria Embankment
London EC4Y 0DZ

An Hachette UK Company
www.hachette.co.uk
www.hachettechildrens.co.uk

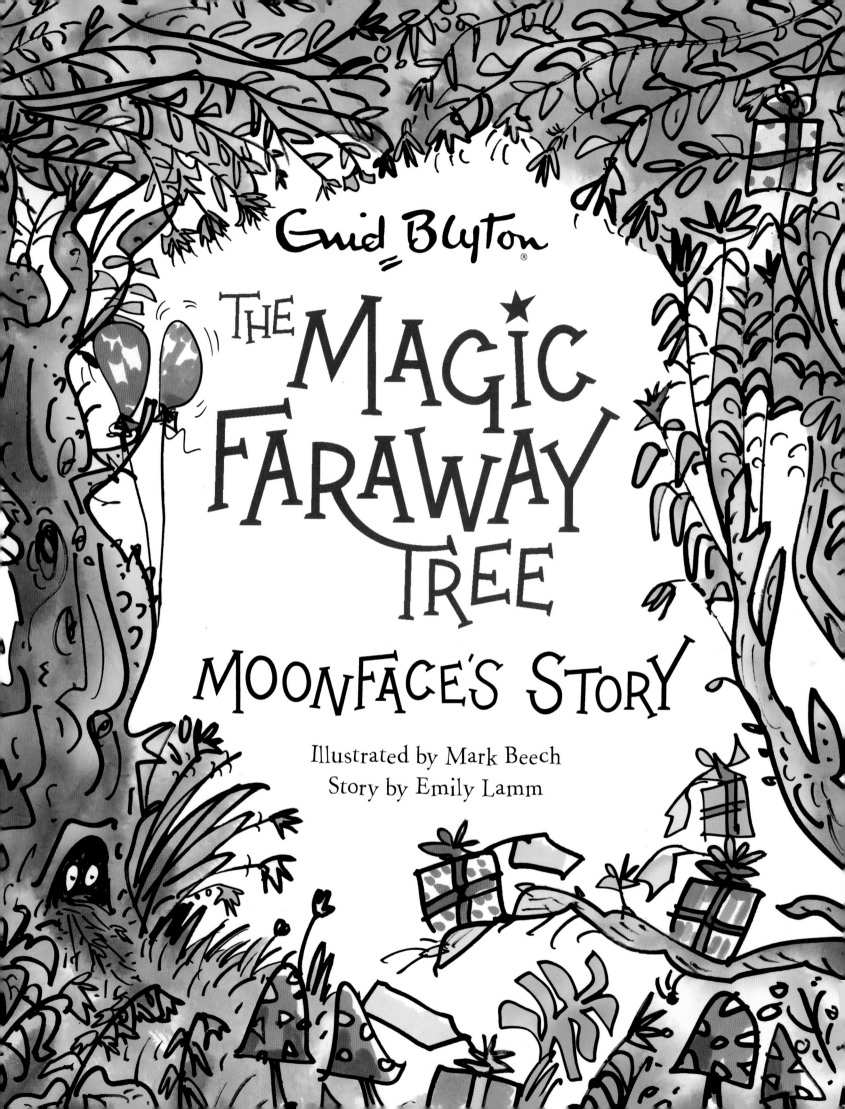

Enid Blyton

THE MAGIC FARAWAY TREE

MOONFACE'S STORY

Illustrated by Mark Beech
Story by Emily Lamm

In the middle of an enchanted wood stood a tree that reached to the clouds. It was called the Magic Faraway Tree and its leaves whispered "wisha-wisha-wisha". It was home to fairies, pixies and other magical creatures.

Near the top lived a kind, friendly man with a beaming smile.

His name was Moonface.

Today was a very special day.
"Happy birthday, Moonface!"
called his friend Silky the fairy, appearing at
his window. "Are you having a party?"

"Yes, and here is your invitation," said Moonface. "It's going to be such
fun. There will be google buns, toffee shocks, ice cream and lemonade!"

"Will there be cake?" asked Silky. "I love cake!"

"Cake?" Moonface frowned for a moment. He hadn't thought of that. "Oh yes, a party must have cake! Thank you, Silky!"

As Silky flew away, Moonface heard a loud clatter. It was Saucepan Man, who wore pots and pans from head to toe. They made such a noise!

"Happy birthday, Moonface!" cried Saucepan Man. "Are you having a party?"

Moonface handed him an invitation. "Yes! There will be google buns, toffee shocks, ice cream, lemonade . . . and cake," he declared.

"Steak?" asked Saucepan Man as his pans jangled.

"No, CAKE!"

"Oh good! Cake is the best thing in the whole world!
See you later, Moonface."

Once Saucepan Man had gone, Moonface set to work. He mixed sugar, butter, eggs and flour and carefully poured the mixture into a tin. Then he whistled loudly and a little red dragon appeared.

The dragon knew just what to do. "Ready in half an hour!" she said.

"That's just enough time to deliver the rest of these invitations," smiled Moonface, and off he went down the Magic Faraway Tree.

But when Moonface returned home . . .

"I can smell burning!" he gasped. "My cake!"

The little red dragon had fallen asleep. She was snoring loudly and clouds of smoke were pouring from her nostrils. Moonface's cake was covered in soot. Oh! How disappointed his guests would be!

"What am I going to do?" cried Moonface.

"Wisha-wisha-wisha,"
went the leaves of the Magic Faraway Tree.
"Wisha-wisha-wisha."

And suddenly Moonface had an idea . . .

At the very top of the Magic Faraway Tree there was a ladder.
It led up through the clouds to a magical land above. You could never
guess what you would find there, for the land was always changing.

Moonface scrambled up the ladder, through the clouds and . . .

"The Land of Cake!" he beamed. "This is very lucky indeed."

Moonface could see chocolate cakes, cherry cakes, sponge cakes, cream cakes. There were fluffy cloud cakes, shimmering moonbeam cakes, rainbow cakes with colour-changing icing . . . every kind of cake you could possibly imagine.

Just then a baker appeared.

"What kind of cake would you like?" she asked.

Now, that was a very tricky question.

"Silky loves twinkle cake. Saucepan Man prefers chocolate cake. Mrs Wash-a-lot loves lemon cake. The squirrels like hazelnut cake . . ."

"What you need is an everything cake!" declared the baker.
"It has a layer of every flavour."

She waved her wooden spoon
like a wand and . . .

an enormous cake appeared, beautifully decorated with sprinkles and swirls of icing. It was taller than Moonface!

"Thank you!" grinned Moonface.

But a strong wind was blowing and Moonface
knew that the Land of Cake would soon disappear.
He must hurry back to the Magic Faraway Tree.

He began to climb down the ladder.

But every time he took a step – wibble, wobble

– the huge cake swayed from side to side!

Wibble, wobble, sway!

Wibble, wobble, sway!

Until finally ~ wibble, wobble . . .

SPLAT!

The giant cake fell out of his hands and tumbled to the bottom of the tree.

"Oh, my beautiful cake!" cried Moonface.

His big beaming smile disappeared and tears began to roll down his cheeks.

Soon there was a clattering sound and Saucepan Man appeared, with Silky the fairy.

Moonface told them about the dragon and the Land of Cake. "It won't be a proper party without cake!" he sobbed.

"Of course it will!" said Saucepan Man. "We'll still have buns and toffee and lemonade."

"And most important of all, you'll still have your friends. That's the best thing about a party," said Silky.

Well, Moonface couldn't help smiling a little at that.

It wasn't long before the rest of Moonface's friends arrived at his house: Mrs Wash-a-lot, Owl, the squirrels, the pixies, Mr Watzisname and Frannie, Joe and Beth, the children who lived near the Enchanted Wood.

"Happy birthday, Moonface!" smiled Beth. "We have something special for you."

"It's a toffee surprise cake!" said Joe. "Your favourite!"

"Oh!" Moonface grinned with delight. "We will have cake after all!"

The friends ate toffee surprise cake, drank lemonade,
played silly games and sang funny songs, long into the night.
What a noise they made! Even the leaves joined
in, whispering, "wisha-wisha-wisha".

And everyone agreed that it was the best party they had ever been to.

So, next time you're in the Enchanted Wood,
look out for the Magic Faraway Tree.
You'll always be welcome to
join the fun . . . and,
who knows, there might
even be cake!